PUFFIN BOOKS

Hamster in Danger

Elizabeth Hawkins lives in London and Dorset. She has written a number of books for children of all ages and she also teaches and lectures on writing for children.

Also by Elizabeth Hawkins

A MONSTER OF A HAMSTER

Elizabeth Hawkins

Hamster in Danger

Illustrated by Ben Cort

PUFFIN BOOKS

To David Hawkins

PUFFIN BOOKS

Published by the Penguin Group
Penguin Books Ltd, 80 Strand, London WC2R 0RL, England
Penguin Putnam Inc., 375 Hudson Street, New York, New York 10014, USA
Penguin Books Australia Ltd, 250 Camberwell Road, Camberwell, Victoria 3124, Australia
Penguin Books Canada Ltd, 10 Alcorn Avenue, Toronto, Ontario, Canada M4V 3B2
Penguin Books India (P) Ltd, 11 Community Centre, Panchsheel Park, New Delhi – 110 017, India
Penguin Books (NZ) Ltd, Cnr Rosedale and Airborne Roads, Albany, Auckland, New Zealand
Penguin Books (South Africa) (Pty) Ltd, 24 Sturdee Avenue, Rosebank 2196, South Africa

Penguin Books Ltd, Registered Offices: 80 Strand, London WC2R 0RL, England

www.penguin.com

First published 2000

3

Text copyright © Elizabeth Hawkins, 2000
Illustrations copyright © Ben Cort, 2000
All rights reserved

The moral right of the author and illustrator has been asserted

Made and printed in England by Clays Ltd, St Ives plc

British Library Cataloguing in Publication Data
A CIP catalogue record for this book is available from the British Library

ISBN 0-141-30583-5

Contents

1. Yummy Rock Cakes

Luke Jones poured the sugar into a wire sieve and shook the sieve over the four rock cakes on the kitchen table. They smelt delicious!

Luke had made the rock cakes with his mother when he had got back from school. He'd mixed together the warm-smelling spices and the flour, rubbed in the butter, and sprinkled in the sugar and sultanas. Luke had left them for twenty minutes in the oven and now they were a gorgeous golden colour, with not a single burnt bit on them. The sieved sugar made the rocky peaks glisten with sugar snow.

'Those have turned out well!' said Luke's mother.

Luke picked up a cake, still warm, and sniffed the crumbly, buttery smell.

'Do you think the old folks will like them?'

'They'll love them,' said his mother. 'Why not test one out? You'll still have three left.'

'Mmm . . . yummy!' Luke spluttered, as his teeth bit into the warm bun.

While the buns cooled on the wire cake-rack, Luke settled down to watch television. It was the first episode of the brand new series *Exterminator III*.

'Mmm . . . yummy!' said Luke's father, coming in from work. 'I know a good rock cake when I taste one.'

'No, Dad!' said Luke. 'They're for the Harvest Thanksgiving at school tomorrow. We're taking them to the old folks at Hopswood Mansions.'

Before Luke went to bed, he and his mother found an old ice-cream carton, covered it with stripy wrapping paper and put the three rock cakes inside. They sealed the box with shiny cellophane. It looked great!

Next morning, the alarm shrieked beside Luke's bed.

On weekdays and holidays Luke was always the first up, but on school days he got his old sleeping sickness back.

This morning he didn't stay in bed though.

He remembered that it was the Harvest Thanksgiving. The whole class would be free of school for the afternoon, so that they could deliver their harvest food gifts.

'Anna-Louise's mother has just rung from next door,' said Luke's mother at breakfast. 'She wants you to help Anna-Louise carry a cake to school.'

Luke choked on his cornflakes.

Oh no! He'd been trying to keep away from Anna-Louise. Whenever Anna-Louise came, trouble crept after her.

'Anna-Louise's mother has been up most of the night icing a cake for Anna-Louise.'

'Icing a cake all night?' said Luke's

father, peering over his newspaper.

'She's just finished a class in cake
icing at the local college, and she says
this is her showpiece. It's for the
Harvest Thanksgiving.'

2. To School Backwards

Luke hitched his backpack carefully across his shoulders. He didn't want to damage his stripy rock-cake package at the bottom.

Ding-dong, chimed the bell on Anna-Louise's shiny green front door.

The door opened a crack. An eye peered out next to the 'NO HAWKERS, NO VENDORS, NO

CANVASSERS, NO CALLERS
WITHOUT APPOINTMENT' sign.

'Oh, it's you, Luke.' The door
widened to reveal Anna-Louise's
mother in a pink apron, with not a stain
or a crease.

'I hope you've got clean hands, Luke.
It's unhygienic to handle cakes without
clean hands. Let me see.'

'They are clean,' protested Luke,
hiding his hands behind him.

Anna-Louise wasn't allowed to keep a
pet because her mother said pets were
unhygienic. Not even the school
hamster had been allowed in the house.

'Is Anna-Louise ready? Mr Pigott said
we mustn't be late for school today as
it's a special day.'

'Anna-Louise!' shrieked Anna-
Louise's mother. 'Come down at once!

I don't want Luke dawdling in the kitchen in his dirty shoes.'

Anna-Louise's kitchen was the sort of place you were only allowed to walk around in socks in case you made the floor dirty.

'I'm coming, Mummy,' came a muffled voice.

A white box on legs was walking towards Luke. Only a few ginger curls peeping round the edge warned Luke it was Anna-Louise.

'That box is enormous!' said Luke. 'How are we going to carry that? I've already got my backpack.'

'Nonsense, Luke,' said Anna-Louise's mother briskly. 'I've seen you with your backpack *and* a football, and your football boots. One cake box is nothing for a tough, rough boy like you.'

Luke peered into the box. The cake was round and huge. It was covered in white icing and pink curly bits, primrose flowers with silver ball centres, and twirly green leaves.

Luke stared in amazement. No one would notice his rock cakes alongside Anna-Louise's cake.

'All made of icing sugar and marzipan,' said Anna-Louise's mother proudly. 'I didn't finish it till late last night. I'm quite dead with exhaustion, which is why I can't take Anna-Louise to school.'

Anna-Louise's mother was always dead with something, but, strangely, she never seemed to die.

'What are you taking to the Harvest Thanksgiving, Luke?' asked Anna-Louise nervously, as she saw Luke's look of horror.

'Rock cakes.'

'Rock cakes.' A tight laugh escaped from Anna-Louise's mother. 'Did you say "rock cakes"?'

'I made them myself,' said Luke indignantly.

'You are lucky,' said Anna Louise.

'I've never made rock cakes . . . or cooked anything myself.'

'Certainly not,' said Anna-Louise's mother. 'I'll not have children messing around in my kitchen. Now carry the box carefully. That's right, Luke. You take the end. You can walk backwards to school.'

It was difficult walking to school backwards without bumping into anyone. At the same time, Luke had to hunch his shoulders to stop his backpack falling off.

'I'm sorry, Luke,' came the muffled voice from the other end of the box. 'I didn't know the cake would be this big.'

'It's huge,' said Luke crossly. 'There wasn't a cake as big as this in my mum's recipe book.'

'It's a wedding cake, Luke. Mummy said she must start practising for my wedding.'

'But you won't be married for years and years and years,' puffed Luke.

'I know, Luke. And what will I do if no one wants to marry me? Mummy will die of disappointment. Will you marry me, Luke, if no one else wants to?'

'Don't be stupid, Anna-Louise.'

Marry Anna-Louise? Certainly not!

Anna-Louise had been born good, like everyone else, at least so Luke reckoned, but unlike everyone else, she had never learnt anything different.

Luke knew that because he had lived next door to Anna-Louise since they were both babies.

Anna-Louise never pinched people or

borrowed things without asking, or said
unkind things about other children.
This was odd enough, but oddest of all,
despite this goodness, Anna-Louise was
always getting into trouble – and getting
Luke into trouble too!

And here it was approaching them already – double trouble!

The terrible twins, Delia and David, each holding a very small plastic bag, had spied Luke and Anna-Louise struggling along with the box.

3. Twins and Trouble

'What's in that box?' Delia asked.

'I can't see,' said David. 'Hold the box lower.'

David pushed down Luke's arms.

Anna-Louise hadn't heard. She was still holding the box high at the other end. The cake slid forward in the box with a thud.

'Look what you've made me do,'

shouted Luke. 'Anna-Louise's cake is all squashed on my side.'

At Luke's end of the cake, the white icing was like a bumpy toboggan run. The primrose flowers had crashed down into the crumpled green leaves, and the silver balls were rolling round the bottom of the box. But peeping through the squashed mess was an edge of scrumptious yellow cake.

'Oh, no!' moaned Anna-Louise. 'Mummy will die when she finds out. She spent hours on this cake.'

Delia smiled her innocent baby smile. (The twins looked alike. They both had shiny blond hair and baby blue eyes. With their wide smiles and big eyes they looked so innocent that no grown-up would believe the terrible behaviour they were capable of.)

'I know what we'll do,' said Delia.

Out of her school bag she pulled a ruler.

'We can use this as a knife. We'll cut off the squashed bits and no one will know.'

And before Luke or Anna-Louise could put down the box, Delia had carved off the squashed end of the cake.

David scooped the squashed pieces out of the box.

'What are we going to do with the bits?' asked Anna-Louise.

What a stupid question! thought Luke, as David and Delia gulped down the squashed pieces of cake and smacked their lips.

A wicked grin spread across their sticky faces.

'Right, Anna-Louise!' said Luke furiously. 'Put down your end of the box when I say "ready" . . .'

But Anna-Louise had already dropped her end.

'You didn't wait, Anna-Louise,' yelled Luke. 'I was going to say "ready".' Luke frowned at David and Delia. 'You should have asked Anna-Louise first before cutting the cake. And if you weren't so greedy we could all have shared the bits.'

David and Delia grinned happily and licked their lips.

'Help yourselves, then,' said David. 'Look, Anna-Louise's end is all squashed and broken now too.'

Luke and Anna-Louise stared down at the battered cake.

Horrors!

The icing was now a toboggan run at Anna-Louise's end, and a delicious hint of yellow sponge poked through the white bumps.

They couldn't give the old people a beaten-up cake like that.

Silently Luke took the ruler Delia held out to him and cut carefully round all the cracked and squashed bits.

'Have some, Anna-Louise,' said Luke guiltily. 'After all, it's your cake.'

'Do you think I should? . . . Mummy would die if she saw it. Well, just a tiny bit.'

Luke took a piece too. It tasted pretty good: rich sponge, with a gooey jam filling, and meltingly sweet icing.

'There're a few bits in the corner,' said Delia, sticking her head into the box. 'Here, we'll share them.'

They all shared a bit more.

'And I'll just tidy it up on the sides,' added Delia.

It was better than a second breakfast!

By the time Delia had finished her tidying, and all four had sucked their fingers clean, a very odd sight met their eyes.

There, at the bottom of the box, was a small piece of sponge cake. It was not exactly round, nor exactly square, but more zigzag-shaped, with a little piece of dirty icing clinging to the top.

Anna-Louise let out a piercing wail. 'I can't take *that* to the Harvest Thanksgiving! What am I going to do?'

Luke had no idea what Anna-Louise

was going to do, but he wasn't getting involved in this. Oh, no! His rock cakes were sprinkled with sugar and not silly icing and were safely wedged in the stripy ice cream box in his backpack.

Luke hadn't asked to transport Anna-Louise's cake all the way to school backwards. He'd been forced into it by Anna-Louise's mother. *This* was Anna-Louise's problem.

4. Into the Bin!

In Class Three of Hopswood Junior School, Mr Pigott was lining up the children with their gifts of food.

'Stand in line, children, while I count you,' boomed Mr Pigott. He always talked far too loud. 'Can . . . you . . . hear . . . me? Now, we are taking our gifts into assembly where we will lay them on the table.'

Mr Pigott stroked his beard as he walked down the line counting the children, 'Sixteen – Samantha, what a lovely bowl of tomatoes. Nineteen – Ben, a tin of sardines, always a favourite! Ali – baked beans, very useful! Those will keep for months in their tin. Twenty-three . . . We're four short. Who's missing?'

All the children turned to watch as four figures crept into the room.

'Late, Anna-Louise! Late, Luke! And, dear me, David and Delia late too. Did I not particularly ask you to be on time today?'

'I was helping Luke with Anna-Louise's cake,' said David, smiling his widest smile.

'And I was helping Anna-Louise tidy her cake up,' said Delia, blinking her blue eyes.

'How very kind of you, twins,' said Mr Pigott. 'And how thoughtless of Luke and Anna-Louise to make you late. Now get into line, and, Anna-Louise, you had better stand at the back with that very big box, next to the hamster cage.'

As Mr Pigott walked up to have a

look inside, the class line broke and all
the children gathered round the
box.

Mr Pigott stared down into the box,
his eyes wide in astonishment.

'Anna-Louise, how could you?'

'It was difficult carrying it,' began
Anna-Louise. 'But . . .'

'How could you have brought such a
horrid, broken, dirty bit of cake?' Mr
Pigott's voice rose in a squawk and his
arms were flapping like some bird that
had forgotten how to fly. 'I see. You
forgot to tell your mother about Harvest
Thanksgiving and so you sneaked off
with that miserable specimen of cake
left over from your tea. Anna-Louise,
would it not have been wiser to come
empty-handed?'

'No, it wasn't like that,' tried Luke.

'I saw the cake. I helped carry the box . . .'

But Mr Pigott wasn't listening now. His arms were flapping so much he looked as if he was about to take off.

'So Luke, *you* brought this ridiculous, great box. I might have known you were behind this, encouraging Anna-Louise.'

Mr Pigott turned to Anna-Louise and stroked his beard.

'If you had forgotten about our Harvest Thanksgiving, Anna-Louise, I am sure Samantha would have given you a tomato.'

Samantha clutched her bowl of tomatoes tightly to her and scowled at Anna-Louise.

Mr Pigott picked up the dirty yellow bit of sponge and threw the last remnant of Anna-Louise's mother's wedding cake into the rubbish bin.

Mrs Harrington, the headteacher of Hopswood Junior School, stood straight-backed in her best grey suit on the platform in the school hall. Behind her was a long dinner table, bending under the weight of tins of custard and peaches, fresh tomatoes and carrots, boxes of tea, biscuits and baskets of apples.

'What a wonderful display of food we have to be thankful for!' said Mrs Harrington.

The children sang a song about rain falling on the harvest while Mr Pigott played his guitar.

Mrs Harrington said how lucky they were to have enough to eat, and how

grateful they should be to the farmers
and the food-manufacturers.

'So this afternoon, we will take our
food gifts to the old folk at Hopswood
Mansions, who will welcome these extra
treats and the chance to chat with well-
behaved, polite children.'

'What am I going to take?' sniffed
Anna-Louise next to Luke.

With a frown at Anna-Louise, Mrs Harrington continued: 'Old people often live alone. Their children have grown up and moved away. They can be lonely. Many have pets for company, but in Hopswood Mansions the Council does not permit pets, so they will enjoy a visit from you. Now . . .' and here Mrs Harrington's cool grey eyes swept over each child, 'I expect the very best, perfect behaviour!'

Back in the classroom, Luke said reluctantly, 'I suppose you could have a rock cake, Anna-Louise. But I've only got three.'

'Don't lend Anna-Louise anything,' said Delia fiercely. 'She'll probably lose it.'

'You're right,' said Luke. 'I think I'll keep them.'

'Luke, stop disturbing Delia and get on with your writing,' boomed Mr Pigott. 'Any bad behaviour and you will not be going to Hopswood Mansions this afternoon.'

'Don't worry, Luke,' whispered Anna-Louise. 'I've just thought of something much better to take.'

5. Miss Grundy

Luke sat down next to Ali to eat his packed lunch. Thank goodness Anna-Louise had disappeared to share her lunch with the class hamster. He was glad to be rid of her.

'Did you see *Exterminator III* on telly last night?' said Ali, crunching his crisps.

'Yes,' said Luke. 'It was really scary.'

'I think those giant-legged beetles from planet Zintos are going to invade the world, don't you?'

'I don't know. I hope the Exterminator finds a way of getting rid of them. If he doesn't, I don't know how I'll bear to watch the next episode.'

'It's on Monday,' said Ali. 'I told my mum I'm going to rush home after school on Monday. I don't want to miss episode two.'

'Good idea,' said Luke. 'I'll do the same.'

'Ali and Luke!' A voice boomed behind Luke. It was Mr Pigott. 'Put away your lunch boxes and collect your Harvest Thanksgiving gifts. You two can be partners for our visit to Hopswood Mansions. Samantha and

Ben, you will be partners, and . . .'

Mr Pigott soon had the class lined up in a crocodile with their partners. The children were carrying baskets of fruit, tins of sweetcorn, flapjacks in old margarine tubs, potatoes in plastic bags. It was a walking feast.

'Where is Anna-Louise?' boomed Mr Pigott. 'Anyone seen Anna-Louise?'

Anna-Louise popped up from behind the table at the back of the class. Her face was red and her arms were clasped round her waist, beneath her school sweatshirt.

'You look very hot, Anna-Louise,' said Mr Pigott, staring at her as she clasped her stomach. 'Have you got a stomach-ache?'

Anna-Louise shook her head.

'You can't stand alone at the back,

Anna-Louise. Come along to the front.
You've nothing to take, I know, but I am
sure Luke will give you one of his rock
cakes. Now, Ali, you join David and
Delia instead.'

Luke was furious! He had been
looking forward to discussing with Ali
how the Exterminator could get rid of

the galactic beetles. Why did everyone think that because he and Anna-Louise lived next door to each other they were best friends?

As the crocodile wound its way out of the playground, Luke ignored Anna-Louise's timid smile.

Hopswood Mansions was a low block of red-brick flats. Along the flats, on each storey, a walkway led to the stairs.

Mr Pigott took the children up to the second floor. He consulted his list.

'Luke and Anna-Louise, you can visit Miss Grundy in flat 204. She has been told by her church that you will be calling today. Now remember, children, your very best manners!'

Luke felt nervous as he raised the shiny knocker on the front door. Anna-

Louise was hopping about rather uneasily too.

The lace curtain at the window edged back, and a little wrinkled face pressed against the glass.

After a lot of rattling of keys and pulling back of bolts, the door at last opened.

'The children from Hopswood Junior School!' said a little old lady with snow-white hair and orange fluffy slippers. 'Come in, come in. How nice to have visitors!'

Luke and Anna-Louise walked into a room covered in lacy material. There were lacy net curtains at the window, lacy white drapes on the chairbacks, lacy white cloths on a table and stool, and even a lacy cover for the television.

'We've brought you our Harvest Thanksgiving gift,' said Luke.

'What's that, dear? A lift? I don't use it. It's always breaking down.'

'No, gift,' shouted Luke. 'We've brought a gift – three rock cakes.'

'Three socks, did you say, dear? But I

don't wear socks. I like warm woolly tights. And three socks are not much good. That's one sock without a partner.'

Luke gave up and held out his stripy ice cream carton with the three sugary rock cakes inside.

The little old lady peered in.

'Oh dear, no,' she said. 'No, I'm afraid not. Definitely not. Those are rock cakes. Can't eat those with old teeth. Much too hard, rock cakes.'

'They only *look* like rocks,' said Luke desperately. 'They're not really hard. They're made of butter and flour and sugar.'

But the old lady sank back into a lacy chair with a disappointed sigh.

'I can't eat them, and that's that,' she said. 'Now if you had brought me a custard tart that would have been another matter. Soft pastry with creamy custard inside.'

Luke stared at his glistening rock cakes, laughed at by Anna-Louise's mother, rejected by Miss Grundy. They didn't know what they were missing.

But at least he could eat them himself on the way home.

'What a disappointment,' went on the old lady, 'and I was so looking forward to your visit. It's not often I have visitors and I get very lonely. What's that you've got, dear?'

Anna-Louise was holding out a handful of squirming orange-brown fluff.

The old lady sat up and stared. Then a big smile spread over her face, making her wrinkles disappear as if by magic.

She held out her hands and took the squirming . . . hamster!

Luke couldn't believe his eyes. But there was no doubt about it. Anna-Louise had brought the class hamster along, stuffed away inside her sweatshirt.

'My Boodles!' the old lady said. 'Oh, you lovely children! How clever of you to find my Boodles.'

6. Boodles

'You'll be in terrible trouble if Mr
Pigott finds out you've brought the
hamster,' hissed Luke.

The little old lady was so happy
whispering and cooing at the hamster,
watching it run all over her chairs,
laughing as it got tangled in the lacy
cloths that she didn't hear.

'Why, Luke?' said Anna-Louise.

'Mrs Harrington said some old people were lonely because they weren't allowed to keep pets, so I brought the hamster.'

'It was a crazy idea.'

'But you spoilt my wedding cake.'

'Me!' exploded Luke. 'I didn't ask to carry that stupid cake. I was doing you a favour.'

'But I didn't have anything to bring. No one wanted to share and I wanted my own gift. Look, Miss Grundy is really happy!'

Anna-Louise was right. Miss Grundy had freed the hamster from a lacy cloth and was cuddling it close.

'My Boodles. There's my sweet Boodles,' Miss Grundy cooed. 'I'll have one of your rock cakes now, dear boy.'

Eagerly Luke handed Miss Grundy a

sugary cake. She was sure to like it
when she tasted it.

But, no. The rock cake went nowhere
near her mouth. Instead she broke off
chunks, crumbled them in her hand
and fed the crumbs to the hamster.

What a waste!

Luke's sugary, buttery rock cake,
demolished by an animal who was just
as happy to eat any old seeds and nuts.

Soon the hamster's cheek pouches
were puffed up with rock cake.

Miss Grundy stroked the hamster's
head.

'Had a lovely tea then, Boodles?'

The hamster snuggled down in her
hand and fell asleep.

'Shush!' Miss Grundy said. 'Creep
out now, dear children. Boodles is
asleep and we mustn't wake him.'

'We have to take the hamster back,'
said a worried Anna-Louise.

'No! Boodles belongs to me. I lost
him and you've found him,' said Miss
Grundy.

'What are we going to do?' wailed
Anna-Louise to Luke.

'This was your idea,' said Luke.
'Nothing to do with me!'

But Luke felt mean. He hadn't
shared his rock cakes with Anna-
Louise, and Miss Grundy looked so
happy.

'Miss Grundy,' he said. 'Perhaps we
can find the real Boodles for you. How
long ago did you lose him?'

'The winter of 1980, and a very cold
winter it was,' said Miss Grundy,
stroking the hamster's contented head.

'1980! But that's ages ago. Our

teacher says hamsters only live two years.'

'But I *know* this is Boodles. I would know him anywhere, and . . .'

Heavy footsteps pounded along the walkway outside the flat.

'Luke and Anna-Louise,' called Mr Pigott. 'Time to say "goodbye".'

'Off you go, children,' said Miss Grundy happily. 'That's your teacher calling.'

'But we must take the hamster back to school,' wailed Anna-Louise.

'Please, Miss Grundy,' said Luke. 'Anna-Louise will be in big trouble.'

But Miss Grundy had opened the front door on to the passage. Outside stood a beaming Mr Pigott.

'A pleasant visit I hope, Miss Grundy,' boomed Mr Pigott.

'Take these children away,' said the little white-haired lady. 'They've been here quite long enough. They won't leave.'

Mr Pigott's smile faltered.

'They've not been bothering you I hope, Miss Grundy.'

Miss Grundy carefully lifted her hands cradling the sleeping hamster.

'They're disturbing my Boodles,' she said.

7. 'Why Didn't You Tell?'

It was one of those moments when they should have confessed. If they had explained to Mr Pigott what had happened and why Anna-Louise had taken the hamster, he might have been able to persuade Miss Grundy the hamster was not Boodles.

He would have said firmly, 'I'm sorry, Miss Grundy, but this hamster is not

Boodles. This hamster belongs to Class Three of Hopswood Junior School.'

Mr Pigott might have been cross with Anna-Louise, but it would have been over and done with.

'Why didn't you tell Mr Pigott?' Luke whispered furiously to Anna-Louise, as they walked back to school in the crocodile.

Anna-Louise was blinking back tears. 'I didn't think he'd believe us. He doesn't listen. He didn't listen when I tried to tell him about my wedding cake.'

That was true, thought Luke. Mr Pigott had even blamed him when all Luke had done was to help carry the box.

It was meeting David and Delia that

had ruined the cake, but then, Luke thought a bit more, he had enjoyed eating the squashed cake, and he hadn't shared his rock cakes either. Maybe he was to blame a little bit too.

'What are we going to do?' whimpered Anna-Louise.

'We'll think of something,' said Luke doubtfully.

Back at school, Anna-Louise and Luke volunteered to fill up the hamster's tray with seeds and water for the weekend.

David and Delia watched Luke fetch the water and fill up the nut and seed tray.

'There's no point doing that,' said David.

'We've checked,' said Delia. 'The hamster's gone.'

'The cage door was open when we got back from Hopswood Mansions,' said David.

'I saw Anna-Louise feeding the hamster with her lunch. It's not allowed,' said Delia, grinning wickedly. 'And she was hiding behind the hamster table before we walked to Hopswood Mansions.'

'Where have you put the hamster, Anna-Louise?' said the twins together.

Anna-Louise and Luke should have told Mr Pigott, but they were afraid to. Now they had to tell the terrible twins, but they didn't want to.

'. . . so Miss Grundy thinks the hamster is her lost Boodles,' sobbed Anna-Louise.

'And Boodles disappeared years and years ago,' explained Luke.

'Wow!' said David.

'Cripes!' said Delia.

'The best thing to do, Anna-Louise,' said Luke sensibly, 'is to tell your mum. Mums are good at sorting out difficult problems.'

'Not Mummy,' said Anna-Louise. 'She hates hamsters. She thinks they're dirty rats and shouldn't be allowed in the classroom. I expect she'd say, "Good riddance".'

'And the cake?' said David, licking his lips.

Anna-Louise's mouth dropped open in horror. 'Oh, no! I'd have to tell her about the wedding cake. She'd die.'

'Did you say a hamster is a rat, Anna-Louise?' said David.

'That's what Mummy says. She hates rats, mice, spiders and beetles. She won't let me watch *Exterminator III* on telly. It makes her nervous.'

'That's interesting,' said Delia. 'No one wants rats in their home, do they?'

8. A Plague of Rats

Luke threw his backpack on the kitchen floor. What a relief to be home!

Tomorrow was Saturday. No one would be in school to miss the hamster for two whole days. That was plenty of time to work out how to get the hamster back.

'Hang up your bag, Luke,' said his mother as usual. 'Did you have a good day visiting the old folk at Hopswood Mansions?'

'Sort of,' said Luke, helping himself to butter and jam to spread on a rock cake.

His mother looked at the two rock cakes and looked at him.

'You've got some rock cakes left?'

'Yes,' said Luke, gloomily munching. 'Do you want a bite, Mum?'

'There's nothing I'd like more.'

In the house next door, Anna-Louise's mother said: 'Was my wedding cake admired?'

'Yes, Mummy. Luke and David and Delia thought it was delicious.'

'How did they know? Did the old folk say the cake icing was exquisite?'

'Well,' said Anna-Louise, blushing. 'It

was kind of sticky . . . and . . .'

'That reminds me, Anna-Louise. I found a sticky toffee-paper under your bed. You will go upstairs now, tidy your room and vacuum under your bed.'

A big girl was in the telephone box chatting for ages to her boyfriend, so David and Delia had to wait.

'You're late home,' said their mother.

Early the following morning, Luke's sleeping sickness had disappeared. He jumped out of bed. It was the weekend and his parents were still asleep. He went down to the kitchen to pour himself a bowl of cereal and turned on the television.

After his cereal he got out his Lego box and began building a racing car.

'And that's cartoons over for now, kids.'

The jokey young man was replaced by a solemn-faced lady who read the news. After the weather, another lady said, 'And now, over to Television Hopswood for the local news. A plague

of rats has been spotted in one of Hopswood Council's blocks of flats for the elderly. Television Hopswood, reliably informed of this disgraceful infestation, has notified the Council Health Department. In the studio we have Councillor Pemberton, Chairman of Housing. Councillor, is this not a disgrace that elderly citizens are living in such filthy, vermin-infested conditions?'

Luke dropped his racing car and listened.

'Indeed, quite shocking!' said the deep voice of Councillor Pemberton. 'Why, only yesterday, the children of Hopswood Junior School visited. We are sending in our Vermin Extermination Service today. We will not rest until the problem has been eliminated.'

Councillor Pemberton had hardly finished before there was a loud banging on Luke's kitchen door.

'Luke! Let me in!' came the wail. 'I know you're up. I can hear the television.'

Luke unlocked the door.

It was raining outside. There, shivering in her nightie, with bare muddy feet, stood Anna-Louise.

'Did you hear that, Luke? Those rats will kill the hamster. What are we going to do?'

Trust Anna-Louise to get it wrong, thought Luke. 'But the hamster *is* a rat,' he said.

'Oh, no!' Anna-Louise let out a shriek. 'Then the hamster will be exterminated.'

'We'll rescue it,' said Luke bravely.

'Go back home and get dressed. Be quick. If your mother catches you in her kitchen with muddy feet, she'll probably exterminate you too.'

9. Too Late!

Anna-Louise was right, thought Luke. If a hamster was a sort of rat it would be exterminated too. How did you exterminate a rat?

Losing the class hamster to Miss Grundy was bad enough, but being responsible for its murder was terrible.

They had no choice. They would

have to go and steal back the hamster before the exterminators arrived.

'Dad, Mum,' said Luke as he stood at his parents' bedroom door. 'There's a plague of rats at Hopswood Mansions. Anna-Louise and I are going to see if Miss Grundy needs help.'

There was a snore from Luke's father. His mother sat up.

'Rats?' She blinked. 'Horrible! But if you think you should go . . . Be careful crossing the road with Anna-Louise. Bring Miss Grundy back here if she wants and if you're not back by ten o'clock we'll come and fetch you.'

Luke's mother fell straight back on to the pillow and fell fast asleep.

Unlike Luke's parents, Anna-Louise's mother was already up, wiping off the

mysterious muddy footprints on her
kitchen floor.

'Mummy,' said Anna-Louise, coming
downstairs fully dressed, 'Luke and I
are going to visit Miss Grundy. There's
a plague of rats at her flats and the
exterminator is going in, so . . .'

'Rats! Those flats must be very dirty,'
shuddered Anna-Louise's mother.

'Don't bring that old lady back here. She might have a rat in her pocket or her handbag. And stay away for an hour. I need to give this floor a good shine with my liquid wax and I don't want anyone walking on it.'

Luke and Anna-Louise raced up the hill to Woodside Avenue. Anna-Louise was quite out of breath trying to keep up with Luke.

'You're going too fast, Luke. I can't . . . Oh! Look at that!'

There, in front of Hopswood Mansions, was a large coach, two vans and a crowd of people. A red van said

HOPSWOOD COUNCIL HEALTH DEPARTMENT VERMIN EXTERMINATION UNIT.

Out of the van climbed two men in red overalls, red boots and masks. From the back of the van they unloaded red tubs labelled '**POISON**'.

A second white van had '**HOPSWOOD TELEVISION**' along its side. A man in a baseball cap was unloading a large camera on wheels, while a lady in a smart trouser suit was tapping a crackling microphone pinned to her jacket.

'We're too late,' said Anna-Louise tearfully. 'The hamster will be poisoned!'

Anna-Louise was right. If only they had got there earlier!

'Look, there's Miss Grundy,' Luke pointed.

Along the balcony walkway and out across the grass came a procession of

old folks, some sprightly, some limping, some leaning on walking sticks or a helper's arm, but each carrying a bag or small case.

At once the television cameras started whirring and the lady reporter began to speak.

'Forced from their homes by a plague of rats, these desperate pensioners . . .'

Luke grabbed Miss Grundy by the arm and took her bag.

'Where are you going, Miss Grundy? I'll carry your bag for you. Can I go back and fetch anything from your flat for you?'

'I've got everything I need, thank you very much. We're going to stay at the Victoria Hotel for the night. We're so excited,' said Miss Grundy. 'I haven't had a holiday for years, so I've packed my best dress. And I helped Mr Bludgens next door to choose a tie and I ironed his clean shirt for him. They want us to get out for the night while the Council looks for bats . . . or was it cats?'

'But what about Boodles?' said Luke desperately.

'Poodles? Dogs as well? The Council

won't like that; dogs are not allowed in our flats.'

A helper frowned at Luke and Anna-Louise.

'Run along now, children. You're blocking the way to the coach.'

'Boodles, Miss Grundy!' cried Anna-Louise. 'The hamster.' And she blew out her cheeks until they were fat and bursting like hamster pouches.

'Oh, Boodles!' smiled Miss Grundy. 'Why didn't you say that before? You must be the nice girl and boy who found my Boodles. He's fast asleep in my rubbish bin. He isn't bothered about bats, and cats won't get near him as the bin has a lid. He's had a big meal and I'll be back tomorrow.'

The helper pushed Miss Grundy up the coach steps.

Miss Grundy waved. 'They say the teas are very nice at the Victoria Hotel.'

The coach moved away, full of smiling, waving old folks.

'They have left,' droned the television reporter, 'torn from their homes, each with a small bag of possessions.'

'Luke, you've got Miss Grundy's bag,' said Anna-Louise.

10. Daylight Robbery

Luke stared down at the bag he was holding. It was a zip bag with pink plastic handles, covered in pink roses.

He looked up to glimpse the coach disappearing round the corner of Woodside Avenue.

'Another thing to worry about,' said Luke gloomily. 'I can't do anything about it now. We've got to rescue the hamster first.'

'We can hide Miss Grundy's bag behind those dustbins,' said Anna-Louise, pointing to a clump of dustbins at the side of Hopswood Mansions. 'How are we going to get across the lawn to the flats, Luke? There are too many people.'

'We'll crouch down and crawl behind them,' whispered Luke. 'Everyone's watching the television reporter.'

Luke put Miss Grundy's bag over one shoulder, dropped to his knees and crawled across the lawn with Anna-Louise behind him.

Anna-Louise gave a yelp.

'Don't crawl so close,' hissed Luke. 'Then I won't kick you.'

'It's not that . . . look,' said Anna-

Louise. 'There's David and Delia.'

The reporter's voice drifted across the grass as she spoke to the two shining blond heads beside her.

'And now,' she said, 'we meet the two children from Hopswood Junior School who rang Hopswood Television. During their visit to the flats yesterday, with their Harvest Thanksgiving gifts, these children were

terrified to see a rat. So shocked were they that they informed . . .'

'Look at those big smiles,' said a woman to her friend. 'Aren't they angels!'

'Devils!' Luke muttered under his breath.

He should never have told the twins, never have trusted them! David and Delia would do anything for a bit of attention.

'And where, children, did you see this shocking rat?' the reporter asked, smiling gently at the twins.

David and Delia turned, blinking their blue eyes, and looked straight at Luke and Anna-Louise.

'Oh, no!' groaned Luke.

But then David and Delia swung round and pointed to a flat on the corner, as far away from Miss Grundy's flat as was possible.

The reporter turned, as did all the watching people.

'Quick,' whispered Luke. 'Here's our chance!'

Bent double, Luke and Anna-Louise stumbled across the lawn. They hid Miss Grundy's pink bag behind the dustbins.

Luke's heart was pounding as he grabbed Anna-Louise's hand and tugged her round the building.

'We'll have to crawl along the walkway to Miss Grundy's flat,' he whispered.

The doors of the flats had been left open for the exterminator. They crawled along and then in past Miss Grundy's shiny knocker.

Anna-Louise leaned against the

passage wall, her face as pink as the roses on Miss Grundy's bag.

'Oh, Luke, isn't this exciting!'

'No, it isn't,' said Luke severely. 'If we get caught it will be all your fault. We'll be in terrible trouble.'

They listened. No one was following.

The flat looked different from the flat they had visited the day before. There were bits of lace everywhere, chewed, messed, hanging off cushions, scattered on the floor.

Surely Miss Grundy wouldn't want to keep the hamster now.

'In the kitchen, Miss Grundy said, in the rubbish bucket.'

Rock cake crumbs led a trail through the kitchen to a rubbish bin with holes punched in the lid.

'Open the lid,' said Luke. 'I'll stand close to catch the hamster.'

'I'm frightened,' said Anna-Louise. 'What if there is a real rat in there? It might jump out and bite me.'

'You shouldn't believe everything you hear on telly, my dad says, and you certainly shouldn't believe a story David and Delia made up.'

Anna-Louise lifted the lid with trembling fingers. Luke reached in and, under several lacy layers, found a warm, sleeping hamster.

'It's the hamster,' cried Anna-Louise with delight.

'Sh!'

Luke handed the hamster to Anna-Louise and she pushed it up under her sweatshirt.

'When we get downstairs,' said Luke,

'we can borrow Miss Grundy's bag to hide it away.'

They crept out of the door, down the stairs. All eyes were on the exterminators stacking up a mound of red tubs marked '**POISON**' in front of the flats.

No one saw Luke and Anna-Louise creep away from the dustbins with the pink rose bag.

11. Strange Behaviour

Back at Luke's house, they hid the rose bag behind the garden shed. It was no use leaving the bag in Anna-Louise's garden: her garden was so tidy it would be seen a mile off.

Luke fetched his last rock cake.

He took a bite and then Anna Louise took a bite.

'Mmm!' said Anna-Louise. 'It's lovely.'

They popped the rest of the rock cake, and a cup of water, into the rose bag, so that the hamster wouldn't starve before Monday morning.

That evening, Luke snuggled down on the sofa between his mother and father and watched a comedy show.

'We will be back in five minutes,' said the announcer of Hopswood Television, 'after the local news.'

And there was the lady reporter, standing outside Hopswood Mansions: 'We meet the two children from Hopswood Junior School who rang . . .'

'That's David and Delia!' said Luke's mother. 'Fancy that!'

'But who's that crawling across the lawn behind them with that great bag?' said Luke's father, leaning forward.

'That's a very odd way to behave. And
. . . don't they look familiar?'

Luke sank back into the cushions.

'It's Luke!' said his mother. 'He's
wearing the stripy sweatshirt I bought
him last year at the market. Fancy Luke
being on television! And that's Anna-
Louise. I'd recognize those ginger curls
anywhere.'

'Is that you crawling, Luke?' said
Luke's father. 'Or is it a giant-legged
beetle from planet Zintos?'

Luke and Anna-Louise met David and
Delia walking to school on Monday
morning.

Luke was so angry with the twins that
he wouldn't say 'Hello'.

'You shouldn't be cross,' said Delia.

'We saved the day,' said David.

'Saved the day!' exploded Luke. 'You made up that stupid story about the rats, called up Television Hopswood, and they brought in the council vermin-exterminators. What could be worse?'

'It was sort of true,' grinned Delia. 'A hamster is a sort of rat.'

'And how would you have got into Miss Grundy's flat to rescue the

hamster,' said David, 'if we hadn't got all the old people out of the flats for you? Luke, you shouldn't be cross, you should be down on your knees, crawling to thank us.'

In class, all the children crowded round David and Delia.

'David, you were brilliant.'

'Delia, you looked beautiful on television.'

'Well done, David and Delia,' boomed Mr Pigott. 'What an honour for Class Three!'

Unnoticed at the back, Luke and Anna-Louise unzipped the rose bag and popped the hamster back in his cage.

'Don't you ever, ever dare borrow that hamster again,' whispered Luke severely to Anna-Louise.

'Chattering at the back?' called out Mr Pigott. 'Is it only Luke and Anna-Louise who have no kind words for David and Delia? And Luke, about that bag you're holding, the one with roses on it. Mrs Harrington has asked to see you and Anna-Louise in her office immediately.'

Mrs Harrington sat upright behind a shiny brown desk. Her chill grey eyes swept across Luke's face and held it in an icy stare.

'Miss Grundy told the police her bag had been stolen. There you were, crawling with it across the lawn with Anna-Louise. You can't deny it. It's all there on the television film, bringing disgrace to Hopswood Junior School.'

Luke tried to explain how he'd never

want a bag with pink roses on it and
that he was only carrying it for Miss
Grundy, but the coach had left too
quickly.

'I'll go round straight after school,' he
said, 'and return the bag.'

'Your trouble, Luke, is that you are
unreliable. One can't depend on you.'

'But you can!' broke in Anna-Louise.
'He always helps . . .'

'Quiet, Anna-Louise! I'm talking to Luke,' said Mrs Harrington. 'And I'm not so sure, Luke, that you are a good influence on poor little Anna-Louise. I know you live next door to each other, but I think you should see a little less of her.'

'That's a very good idea,' said Luke with relief.

That afternoon, Miss Grundy was back in her flat, delighted to have her rose bag back.

'Such a shame, I didn't have my best dress for tea at the Victoria Hotel,' said Miss Grundy, 'but Mr Bludgen said my everyday dress looked quite good enough.'

'I'm sorry about Boodles, Miss Grundy,' said Luke.

'Boodles?' said Miss Grundy, surprised. 'You wouldn't know about Boodles. I lost him twenty years ago, way before you were born.'

Miss Grundy had lived so long that sometimes twenty years seemed like yesterday, and at other times what happened two days ago was quite forgotten.

'Thank you for the bag, dear boy,' said Miss Grundy, 'Although I won't be needing it now the exterminators have gone.'

EXTERMINATORS – Monday! He was going to miss episode two!

12. Rock Cakes Again

Luke ran down Woodside Avenue and all the way home.

Waiting outside his house was Anna-Louise.

'It's over,' said Anna-Louise.

'What happened?' panted Luke. 'Did the Exterminator get rid of the giant-legged beetles from Zintos?'

'I don't know. Mummy won't allow

Exterminator on the television. She says it makes her nervous. We had *The Joy of Gardening* instead.'

'So what are you waiting here for?' said Luke angrily. 'I've taken the rose bag back. Mrs Harrington said I was to see less of you.'

'But Mrs Harrington isn't right,' said Anna-Louise. 'You're kind and I always depend on you.'

Luke grunted.

'So, will your mother let me come in and make rock cakes with you?'

'No!'

'But they were so buttery and sugary. They were the best buns I've ever eaten.'

'Well . . . maybe one day.'

'But Mummy never lets me make or cook anything in her kitchen. She says

I'll make a mess. I've never made a rock cake. You can eat them all, Luke, every one, because you were so brave rescuing the hamster.'

And Luke made the mistake of looking into Anna-Louise's brimming green eyes.

'All right,' Luke muttered. 'We'll ask my mum.'

'If I give you all the ones I make,' said Anna-Louise, 'would you lend me one back?'

'We'll share,' said Luke, smiling.